CONTENTS

Hidden in the shadows,
a hero keeps watch.
He is the Caped Crusader
against crime. He is the
Dark Knight of justice.
These are ...

The AMAZING ADVENTURES of
BATMAN™

Chapter 1
MUD NIGHT AT THE MUSEUM

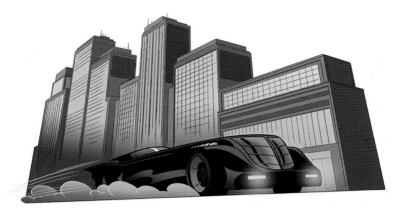

Batman patrols Gotham City in the Batmobile. By his side sits Ace the Bat-hound. Suddenly a police alert comes over the Batmobile's radio. **BEEP! BEEP! BEEP!**

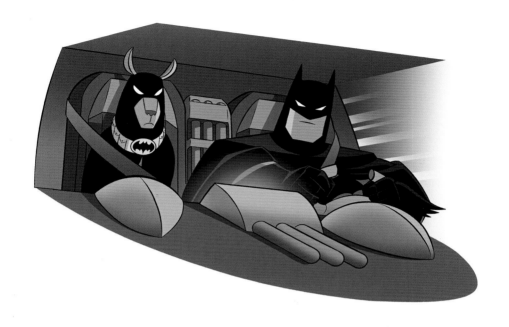

"Calling all units! The Gotham City Museum is being robbed!" a voice on the radio says.

The Dark Knight speeds towards the Gotham City Museum. He and Ace find the museum surrounded by police and firefighters.

Police Commissioner James Gordon walks up to Batman and Ace.

"All the alarms in the museum went off at once," Gordon tells Batman. "We know a robbery is taking place inside, but we don't know where."

"Ace and I will find out," the Dark Knight says.

"Arf! Arf!" Ace agrees.

The super heroes run into

the museum. They quickly

find muddy footprints. Ace

tracks them to the thief.

"Clayface!" Batman says.

The villain holds a large,

pink jewel in his hand. He

swallows the gem and then

leaps at the heroes.

Clayface turns his hands into hammers. He tries to hit Batman and Ace.

WHACK! WHAAAACK!

The heroes dodge the villain's blows.

Chapter 2
MUD FIGHT

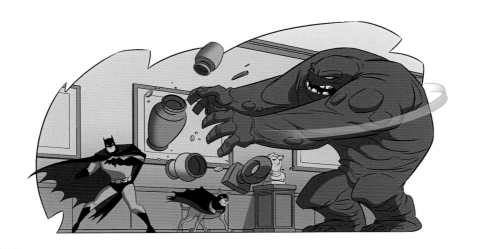

Clayface changes his attack. He starts to throw things at Batman and Ace. The objects are priceless pieces of art.

While the heroes catch vases and statues, Clayface runs into the Dinosaur Hall. A giant model of a Tyrannosaurus rex gives him an idea.

Moments later, Batman

and Ace dash into the

Dinosaur Hall.

ROAAAR!

Clayface has turned into

a giant, muddy T. rex!

Ace chomps the T. rex's tail. Clayface whips his tail to shake Ace loose, but the Bat-hound hangs on.

Batman tosses a Batrope around the mud monster's neck. He uses it to leap onto the T. rex's back. Clayface tries to buck Batman off.

"It's like riding a bucking

bronco," Batman says.

The Dark Knight throws

another Batrope around the

T. rex's snout. He uses it to

guide the monster through

the museum.

Batman steers Clayface towards the museum's front doors. Ace bounces along on the clay dinosaur's tail.

"Hang on," the Dark Knight calls out.

STOMP! STOMP! STOMP!

They lumber through the doors. The heroes ride the T. rex down the museum's steps and onto the street.

Chapter 3

ALL WASHED UP

Batman turns the clay

T. rex towards the police

cars and fire engines. The

flashing lights confuse the

monster. Clayface spins in

circles.

Ace still hangs onto the T. rex's tail. At the same time, he uses one paw to shoot a Bat-grapnel from his Utility Collar.

THWOOONK! The grapnel sinks into the base of the museum.

"Arf! Arf!" Ace barks as he lets go of the T. rex's tail and circles the villain's legs.

The Batrope attached to the grapnel wraps around Clayface's dinosaur legs. **SPLAAAT!** The T. rex falls flat on his back.

Batman jumps off the

dinosaur as the firefighters

spray their water hoses.

"No!" the villain cries as

they melt him down.

Then the police rush up

with super-sized vacuums.

VROOOM! VROOOM!

They suck up Clayface in

his liquid form.

The stolen jewel glitters on the street. Ace fetches the gem and brings it to the Dark Knight.

"Good boy!" Batman says. Then he hands the jewel to Commissioner Gordon.

"Thank you for saving the gem, Batman," Gordon says. "And thank you, Ace, for another amazing adventure!"

BATMAN'S SECRET MESSAGE!

Hey, kids! What was Clayface before he became a super-villain?

1
16 18 15 6 5 19 19 9 15 14 1 12
1 3 20 15 18

Use the code below to solve the Batcomputer's secret message!

1	2	3	4	5	6	7	8	9	10	11	12	13
A	B	C	D	E	F	G	H	I	J	K	L	M

14	15	16	17	18	19	20	21	22	23	24	25	26
N	O	P	Q	R	S	T	U	V	W	X	Y	Z

alert a warning of danger

bronco a wild horse

commissioner an official who heads up a police department

grapnel a grappling hook

patrol to protect and watch an area

priceless relating to something too precious to put a value on

surround to be on every side of something

villain wicked, evil or bad person who is often a character in a story

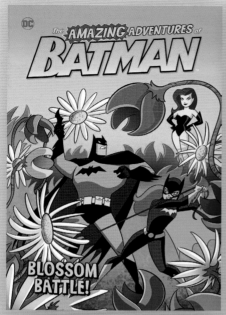

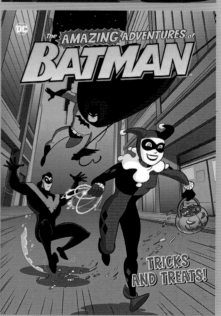

Author

Laurie S. Sutton has read comics since she was a child. She grew up to become an editor for Marvel, DC Comics, Starblaze and Tekno Comics. She has written for series such as Adam Strange for DC, Star Trek: Voyager for Marvel, and Star Trek: Deep Space Nine and Witch Hunter for Malibu Comics. There are long boxes of comics in her wardrobe where there should be clothes and shoes. Laurie has lived all over the world, and currently lives in Florida, USA.

Illustrator

Dario Brizuela was born in Buenos Aires, Argentina, in 1977. He enjoys doing illustration work and character design for several companies including DC Comics, Marvel Comics, Image Comics, IDW Publishing, Titan Publishing, Hasbro, Capstone Publishers and Disney Publishing Worldwide. Dario's work can be found in a wide range of creations including Star Wars Tales, Ben 10, DC Super Friends, Justice League Unlimited, Batman: The Brave & The Bold, Transformers, Teenage Mutant Ninja Turtles, Batman 66, Wonder Woman 77, Teen Titans Go!, Scooby Doo! Team Up and DC Super Hero Girls.